D1581957

Step by Step

By Kathryn Boger, PhD, ABPP
Illustrated by Hiroe Nakata

MAGINATION PRESS ● WASHINGTON, DC
AMERICAN PSYCHOLOGICAL ASSOCIATION

To Brady, Tommy, and Brooks, who have taught their mom
a thing or two about being brave—*KB*

Books for Kids From the
American Psychological Association

Magination Press is a registered trademark of the American Psychological Association.
Order books at maginationpress.org, or call 1-800-374-2721.

Book design by Christina Gaugler
Printed by Worzalla, Stevens Point, WI

Library of Congress Cataloging-in-Publication Data
Names: Boger, Kathryn, author. | Nakata, Hiroe, illustrator.
Title: Step by step / by Kathryn Boger ; illustrated by Hiroe Nakata.
Description: Washington, D.C. : Magination Press, 2023. | Summary: With his mother's help, Sam learns how to face his fears, one small step at a time. Includes a Note to parents and caregivers with more information about helping children face their fears.
Identifiers: LCCN 2023006664 (print) | LCCN 2023006665 (ebook) | ISBN 9781433842412 (hardback) | ISBN 9781433842429 (ebook)
Subjects: CYAC: Anxiety—Fiction. | Self-reliance—Fiction. | Mothers and sons—Fiction. | BISAC: JUVENILE FICTION / Social Themes / Emotions & Feelings | JUVENILE FICTION / Social Themes / Self-Esteem & Self-Reliance | LCGFT: Picture books.
Classification: LCC PZ7.1.B64476 St 2023 (print) | LCC PZ7.1.B64476 (ebook) | DDC [E]—dc23
LC record available at https://lccn.loc.gov/2023006664
LC ebook record available at https://lccn.loc.gov/2023006665

Manufactured in the United States of America

10 9 8 7 6 5 4 3 2 1

Every day, there are new things for Sam to try!
But new things can feel scary.

Sam gets invited to a friend's house.

"No," he says. "I can't go!
What if I don't like it there?"

Sam curls up with his animal.

Mom scoops him up.

"It makes sense that you're feeling afraid. This is new for you.

And I know you can do this. We can take small steps together."

Slowly, Sam gets ready
to leave the house.

In the car, he rolls down the window and feels the wind on his face.
He takes slow, slow breaths like his mom taught him.

When they arrive, they walk to the front porch and wait for a while.

Sam feels his heart beating faster. He asks Mom
if they can wait just a little longer.

When Sam feels more ready, he stands on his tippy toes to ring the bell. It sounds like the wind chimes at his grandma's house.

In the living room, Sam grips his mom's hand as his friend bounds up to him.

Sam's friend asks if he wants to play tag. Tag is Sam's favorite game!

He lets go of Mom's hand.

Step by step, bit by bit,
Sam learns he can handle it.

A few weeks later, Sam visits a farm.

He wants to have fun but the new sounds and smells make him feel afraid.

Sam runs away from the barn and sits on a rock.

Mom catches up to him and kneels down.

"It's ok to feel scared. **And** I know you can do this.
What is the first step you can take?"

Sam thinks for a bit and watches the
fluffy clouds float through the sky.

"I can come down from the rock?"

He takes hold of Mom's hand,
and she gives it a squeeze.

Sam hops to the ground
and slowly heads toward
the barn, picking up
dandelions and
blowing puff balls
into the air.

In the barn, Sam watches the horses
as they swat flies with their tails.

One of the horses makes a silly snuffling sound,
and it makes Sam giggle.

Sam wonders if the horse is hungry. His fingers shake a little as he reaches out and offers her a handful of hay.

The horse gobbles it up.

Step by step, bit by bit,

Sam learns he can handle it.

Soon it's Sam's first day of school.

"I don't think I can go today!
What if I get lost?"

Sam throws the blanket over
his head.

Mom sits on the bed.

"This feels scary. It's your first day.
And I believe in you.
What first step can you take?"

Sam peeks out from under the covers. "I can get out of bed."

Sam stretches his arms and gets out of bed, one little foot at a time.

Mom tousles his hair: "Great idea! And then what?"

Sam brushes his teeth
and splashes cool water on his face.

His stomach swirls as he pulls on his brand new
shirt and the socks with no holes.

Sam and his mom walk to school.
They watch kids scurrying into the building.

Sam's not sure he's ready to say bye just yet.

Sam takes a slow breath and pictures the brave steps he has taken before. He can handle it!

In his new classroom Sam notices the colorful pictures on the walls.

He finds his seat next to a girl with curly hair.
He gives her a little smile, and she smiles right back.

Sam listens to his teacher
and picks up his favorite pencil.
He's ready for the next step.

Sam is learning that there are so many things he can do when he's willing to try things that feel scary and new.

Step by step, bit by bit,

Sam learns he can handle it.

Reader's Note

Sam is a curious and thoughtful child. Sometimes he feels afraid of new situations and wants to avoid them, which is an understandable reaction. When children (and adults) are scared of things, they often want to stay away from them. If Sam avoids things like play dates and school, he'll probably feel relief in the moment. But if this turns into a consistent pattern, Sam's brain will learn to be even more afraid, creating an unhelpful cycle of fear and avoidance. This book is about giving children and parents a new way of responding to things that feel scary, empowering them to approach instead of avoid.

Supporting Children in Facing Their Fears

As adults, when we see children feel afraid, our instincts often tell us to "protect" them by helping them escape or avoid the things that feel scary. As long as there is no true danger (the child is not facing down a bear!), this form of "protection" actually leads to more fear and avoidance over time. In contrast, when adults acknowledge and allow children's feelings with compassion (for example, "This feels scary. It's your first day") *and* support them in slowly facing their fear ("I know you can do this. We can take small steps together"), children feel understood and gain confidence in themselves and in their ability to manage challenges. By doing things that feel scary,

children learn that their worst fears usually don't come true and that, even if they do, they can handle it.

Exposure

The formal name for the strategy of gradually facing fears is exposure. Exposure is a key component of Cognitive-Behavioral Therapy (CBT), a helpful treatment for anxiety disorders. Exposure means doing things that feel scary, such as talking in front of other people, getting a flu shot, or traveling on planes, in a structured and gradual way. A key aspect of exposure is breaking down a feared thing or situation into smaller steps, starting with easier steps and moving to more challenging ones. When Sam was feeling afraid of going to school, he took a bunch of small steps (getting out of bed, traveling to school, and waiting outside the school with his mother), each of which could be considered an exposure.

If another child were afraid of something else, such as dogs, they, too, could tackle their fear through a series of exposures. They could start by saying the word "dog" several times. They would practice this over and over until their brain learned that it was safe and that they could handle it. Then they could look at pictures of different types of dogs, again over and over, until they felt less afraid. As a next step, they could watch cartoon clips of dogs doing silly things, then they could practice watching videos of *real* dogs doing funny things. Next they might move on to looking at their neighbor's dog from across the street. After that, they could pet a dog and eventually play with a dog they know.

This can be a bumpy process and doesn't always go as smoothly as it did for Sam. Some children may benefit from including more steps for a slower transition. One of the great things about exposure is that it's completely customizable; you can take whatever number of steps, at whatever speed, works for your child.

Empathy and Encouragement

You can support a child who is feeling afraid of something by empathizing with their feelings *and* encouraging them to face their fear in a step-by-step manner. A key part of this process is praising the child for the effort they put into taking each brave step. Some kids benefit from getting small prizes, such as stickers, for the steps that they take. Just remember that the more attention you give to the brave behaviors, the more they will happen.

Putting the Steps Together

1. Help your child identify what is making them feel afraid.

2. Empathize with their feeling ("It sounds like you are feeling really scared").

3. Help your child break down the feared thing or situation into smaller steps.

4. Encourage your child to take the first step.

5. Empathize with how hard this feels, if they are struggling.

6. Praise your child for their effort.

7. Move to the next step when your child is ready.

8. Keep practicing!

Questions to Ask Your Child as You Read this Book Together:

1. What did you learn from Sam about doing things that feel scary?

2. Is there something you are afraid to do right now?

3. What is one small step you can take toward doing that scary thing? Let's brainstorm together.

4. How can I help you feel more ready to take this step?

How to Know if Your Child Needs More Support

It's normal for children to feel afraid sometimes. Things like fear of the dark and monsters are typical, and it's common for children to feel nervous about trying new things. But if your child's fear is frequent, is causing them to get very upset, or getting in the way of things that matter to them, like going to school, participating in activities they enjoy, or interacting with friends or family, consider asking for help. As a starting place, you could call the number on the back of your insurance card or ask your pediatrician for referrals to a therapist who has training and experience in evidence-based treatment (meaning treatment that is backed by research), such as CBT.

Kathryn Dingman Boger, PhD, ABPP, is a board-certified child and adolescent clinical psychologist who has devoted her career to helping children and teens with anxiety and Obsessive-Compulsive Disorder. In 2013, she co-developed the McLean Anxiety Mastery Program (MAMP) at McLean Hospital. She was also an Assistant Professor in Psychology at Harvard Medical School and has published peer-reviewed journal articles, delivered regional and national talks (including a TEDx), and provided training to hospitals, schools, and the community. In 2021, Dr. Boger co-founded InStride Health with the mission of increasing access to insurance-backed, research-based care for children, adolescents, and young adults with anxiety and OCD. She lives in Massachusetts.

Hiroe Nakata graduated from the Parsons School of Design. Illustrations from her first children's book were chosen for the Society of Illustrators Annual Exhibition. She lives in Tokyo, Japan.

Magination Press is the children's book imprint of the American Psychological Association. APA works to advance psychology as a science and profession and as a means of promoting health and human welfare. Magination Press books reach young readers and their parents and caregivers to make navigating life's challenges a little easier. It's the combined power of psychology and literature that makes a Magination Press book special. Visit maginationpress.org and @MaginationPress on Facebook, Twitter, Instagram, and Pinterest.